THE CA

A BURNING QUESTION

ONE

Dense smoke cast a pall across Tonbridge at seven o'clock that morning.

It stained the air, wisps tumbling on the breeze and creating a white haze over the jumbled buildings that jostled for space along the main street.

Cars slowed while suit-clad pedestrians shifted black canvas backpacks, handbags or sports holdalls from one shoulder to the other and frowned while they crossed the painted metal bridge spanning the River Medway on their way to the train station at the far end of the road.

A glow rose beyond the high street now, claiming the frigid winter's day, a portent of destruction that grew with every passing second.

For once, the commuters ignored the bird shit that clung to the railings and forgot to wrinkle their noses in disgust at the flaking paintwork, and instead wondered what was on fire.

Sirens wailed now, drawing closer, and people

craned their necks as one in time to see two fire engines tear through the junction at the far end of the road before disappearing, the roar from the engines carrying to where the bystanders gawped at each other, and then the fire-flecked horizon.

A woman in her forties, her razor-sharp tailored suit trouser hems dangling elegantly over ankle boots with three-inch spike heels, squinted through the smoke to the far reaches of the winding river and placed her hand on her companion's arm.

'Is that the boatyard?'

He looked up from his phone, shook his floppy fringe from his eyes and squinted to where she pointed. 'God, I hope not. The whole bloody lot could go up, and my sister's house is down there.'

Their pace slowed while they stared, the sound of a third set of sirens streaming towards them.

Then it was gone, dashing between the houses to reach its target.

The couple checked their watches, he shrugged and then gave her an apologetic smile.

'We'll be late.'

'We should be going.'

A cyclist zipped along the concrete path alongside the river towards the street, his luminescent lycra top at odds with the sombre weather and tainted sky. He zig-zagged between a pair of middle-aged joggers before reaching the pavement and expertly unclipped from his pedals while waiting for the pedestrian lights to change in his favour.

He caught the eye of the woman, jerked his head over his shoulder and lowered his voice conspiratorially.

'There's a boat on fire, down near the sports field.'

Her eyebrows shot upwards. 'What happened?'

The cyclist shrugged, the catastrophe already old news as he contemplated the queue outside the franchised coffee shop a couple of hundred metres away. 'Don't know. I expect it'll be online later.'

They parted ways, him resting his shoes on the pedals while he glided down the slight incline towards the café and the couple reluctantly turning away from the spectacle to hustle past the closed restaurants, determined to catch the seven-thirty service to London Bridge.

And find a seat for the journey, if they were quick.

Detective Constable Kay Hunter watched them go, then pulled up the collar of her padded coat and shoved her hands in her pockets despite the pale blue sky that penetrated the burgeoning smoke in places.

A stiff wind lifted her fringe, and she buried her lips within the soft woollen scarf that was bundled around her neck before turning at the sound of footsteps.

'Hell of a way to start a shift.'

'Hell of a way to start a morning, especially for that boat owner.' She fell into step beside DC Richard Christie, easily matching his long stride. 'How was your weekend?'

RACHEL AMPHLETT

'Quiet. Not that I'm complaining. Sadie's parents had the kids over on Saturday night.' He sidestepped an older couple with a small rat-like dog with a nod of recognition, then gave Kay a rueful smile. 'We were planning on going out for a romantic dinner but by six o'clock we decided a night in front of the TV with a takeaway pizza sounded more fun. Am I officially old now?'

'Not yet. Did you ask her?'

Colour rose to his cheeks. 'I chickened out.'

'Richard…'

'I know. I will ask her. I just have to wait for the right moment, and that's not while we're watching a bad movie with lukewarm pizza.'

Kay laughed, then spotted a familiar figure a few hundred metres ahead and her good mood quickly dissipated. 'There's the guv.'

Detective Sergeant Devon Sharp held up a hand to the driver of a luxury four-by-four who braked to a standstill, then jogged across two lanes of traffic to join them, his brow furrowing when he saw Kay. 'You didn't drive?'

'In this, Sarge?' Kay snorted, indicating the nose-to-tail traffic clogging the street. 'Not likely. Besides, I only live twenty minutes away. I was on my way out the door when you called.'

'Same here.' Christie turned and led the way down a side street that curled around towards the river, then called over his shoulder. 'So, what do you think, Sarge? Have we got an arsonist on our hands?'

Sharp's face turned grim, his pace quickening. 'Three boats in six weeks? Hell of a coincidence.'

'No such thing as coincidence,' Kay murmured.

'Exactly, Hunter. Exactly.'

TWO

A pungent stink of rotting vegetation clung to the riverbank, redolent of autumnal debris and seasons past.

Smoke shrouded the muddy footpath that was cluttered with snaking hoses and other fire-fighting equipment, shouts carrying across to where Kay and her colleagues waited, mindful to stay out of the way until the all-clear was called.

She glanced over her shoulder to the boatyard farther along the towpath and exhaled.

At least the fire hadn't taken hold on any of the vessels lining the path at that end. The result would have been apocalyptic with the right mooring arrangements there.

Murky water rippled around the hulls of the boats beside her. There was a steady flow to the river and the level high after the weekend's deluge while green mould clung to the paintwork of the nearest cabin cruiser, the curtains drawn and yellowing with age. An old fishing rod and a tackle box were the only items on the deck, and Kay wondered how many of the boats along here were habitable on a long-term basis.

Turning back to the source of the acrid stink swirling in the air, she saw two uniformed constables standing beside a patrol car beyond a pair of lowered steel bollards at the far end of the lane abutting the river. Their heads were bowed while they listened to a woman swaddled in a woollen blanket, one of them with a notebook in his hand.

Photographs fluttered and tumbled on the breeze as a probationary constable did her best to gather them up, and another junior officer shoved the meagre clothing that had been salvaged from the blaze into a black plastic bin liner.

'Thank god she got out,' Kay murmured. She cast her gaze over the hodgepodge of personal belongings strewn over the bank beside the smoking remains of a forty-foot narrowboat.

'So did the cat,' said Sharp, nodding at a sleek tabby that scrambled out from the blanket wrapped around the woman and landed on the soaking grass.

The cat gave the three detectives a beleaguered glare, then turned and marched off to one of the other boats moored farther downstream, where it promptly skipped on board and sat with its back to them.

'And that's why I'd always have a dog,' said Christie.

'Got a minute?'

They turned at the shout to see a senior fire officer heading towards them, his already bulky frame ballooned by hi-vis protective clothing.

Stomping across the grass in heavy boots, he removed his helmet and ran a hand over sweat-drenched hair. Nodding to Kay and Christie, he turned his attention to the DS. 'Thought you'd want to know as soon as possible – the forensics lot will confirm it in time – but it looks like an accelerant was used.'

'Petrol?' Sharp said, craning his neck to see past the fireman to where the man's colleagues were starting to clear away the equipment.

'Certainly smells like it.' The man thrust out his hand. 'Wayne Matthews.'

'Detective Sergeant Devon Sharp.'

'So, do you think this is the same as the other fires?'

The DS pursed his lips and squinted through the hazy air as the narrowboat's skeleton emitted a sickening groan before dropping several inches into the silty riverbed. 'It's too early to say whether the three fires are connected.'

Kay turned away from the two men, gauging Sharp's cagey response.

They couldn't risk anyone alerting the media to a serial arsonist, not when their investigation was at such a critical stage.

Until this morning, when the call had come through and Sharp had scrambled his team to reach the scene of the fire, nobody in the tiny incident room at Tonbridge had ventured the suggestion that the fires were connected.

Until then, the first fire six weeks ago had been treated as a vengeance attack and the second three and a half weeks ago as an accident.

Until now…

'They'll be baying for us,' Christie muttered beside her. 'And asking why we didn't do something sooner.'

Kay glanced over her shoulder to where Sharp and Matthews were speaking in lowered voices then flapped her stiffening hands from her coat pockets and cupped her fingers to her mouth, blowing hot air across them in a vain attempt to warm up. 'Glad it's not me who's going to be dealing with the media.'

'All right, you two – we've got the all-clear.' The DS beckoned to them. 'Let's take a look, and then you can speak to the owner while I head back to the incident room.'

Following a demarcated path and lifting a fluorescent plastic tape cordoning off the immediate area beside the stricken vessel, Kay trudged behind her colleagues.

A woman in her forties stood beside the boat owner, squeezed her arm and then made her way towards them, pausing at a gate cut into a garden fence next to the towpath.

Sharp aimed a glance over his shoulder to Christie, who paused and let the detective sergeant walk on alone.

'Excuse me, did you know the victim?' Christie already had his notebook out, rummaging under his coat for a moment before extracting a plastic ballpoint pen.

The woman gave a slight nod, then wiped at her eyes. 'After everything she's been through this year, this happens.'

'Sorry, what's your name?'

'Ellie Greening.'

'What do you do?'

'Graphic design. I started up my own freelance business a couple of years ago.'

'What's the owner's name?'

'Briony Peters.'

'Does she have any family members we can call?' Kay asked, her chest aching as she watched the cat trot back towards its owner, its tail high.

'No. Briony and her husband divorced six years ago, and her daughter refuses to speak to her. She moved down from London last year because the mooring fees were getting so expensive. What with that and trying to get her yoga business established in the local area, I don't think she's had much time for making friends yet.'

'You knew her well, then?' Christie prompted.

Ellie gave him a rueful smile. 'We call ourselves "the over-40s and divorced club". I usually pop over to hers or vice versa a couple of times a week. It depends what we've got on.'

'Does she have anyone she can stay with?' said Kay.

'I was just telling her she can have my spare bedroom for as long as she needs it.' The woman peered across to where Briony was wiping at her eyes and swallowed. 'I'll look after her, don't you worry.'

THREE

Kay paused when she reached the patrol car and took a moment to look at the other houses backing onto the river.

An elderly man peered between net curtains in one of the terraced dwellings, his brow knitted together while he watched the second fire engine make its way towards the road. His mouth downturned, he gave a sad shake of his head when he saw Kay before letting the curtains drop back into place, and she made a mental note to speak to him as soon as she got a chance.

Farther along, a woman with a toddler cradled in her arms hovered behind a sturdy fence, her face pale. Kay wandered over and introduced herself.

'I thought it was going to spread,' the woman said in a shaking voice. 'I even packed a bag, just in case. You should've seen the embers in the air before the first fire engine turned up.'

'How long have you lived here, Mrs…?'

'Beckett. Joanne Beckett.' She shifted the little

boy to her other hip, the child twisting his neck to see around them to watch the last of the hoses being coiled away, his face rapt. 'We moved in three years ago, from Crawley. Cormac – my other half – got a job at the hospital in Pembury.'

Kay nodded towards the boat owner. 'Do you know Briony?'

'Not really.' Joanne pulled the toddler's sweatshirt hood over his hair, then shivered. 'I've seen her around of course, and we wave if we spot each other but the boat owners tend to keep to themselves.'

'Any trouble recently?'

'Not that I'm aware of, no.'

'No raised voices or anything like that?'

The woman shook her head.

'Have you seen anyone acting suspiciously around the boats any time in the past few weeks?'

'No, sorry.' Joanne jiggled the toddler in her arms. 'This one keeps me too busy to spend time looking out the window.'

'All right, thanks.' Kay turned away and set off towards Christie, who was now talking to the boat owner.

He broke off when she approached, beckoning her closer. 'This is Briony Peters.'

'Ms Peters? I'm Detective Constable Kay Hunter.'

Briony shrugged the thick blanket up around her neck and peered at her with baleful eyes. 'More questions?'

'Just a few, if you don't mind.'

'I've told your friends over there everything that happened.' She jerked her chin towards the patrol car that was disappearing between the houses.

'It helps us to hear it in your own words as well,' Christie explained gently. 'If that's all right?'

'I suppose so.' Her top lip curled. 'It's not like I'm going anywhere, is it?'

Kay looked beyond her colleague and spotted an old white plastic garden chair that had been tossed over the back fence of one of the properties and now lay upended amongst the weeds verging the river. She strode over, wiped it off with the sleeve of her coat, and then set it down beside Christie. 'Here, Briony – have a seat. You must be exhausted.'

'Thanks.' The woman collapsed into the chair, then wiped at her eyes at the sight of the meagre belongings being put into a cardboard box one of the neighbouring boat owners had brought over. 'Oh, God. What am I going to do?'

A sob wracked her then, and she dropped her face into her hands, her shoulders heaving.

Kay crouched beside her and dug out a tissue from her bag. 'Here. Briony, we're going to do everything we can to find who did this, I promise.'

'Have you received any threats in the past?' Christie said, his voice gruff. 'Has anyone been causing trouble down here lately?'

'A little while ago, yes. Things like door locks being tampered with, mooring ropes being cut...'

'Did you report it?' asked Kay.

Briony shot her a withering look. 'We gave up after the third time. Your lot weren't interested, and no-one even bothered to come and take statements that last time.'

Kay blushed.

'You said "the last time",' said Christie, nonplussed. 'Did the vandalism stop?'

'Until today you mean?' The woman shrugged. 'About four weeks ago. I'd got my insurance sorted out by then, thank goodness. Plenty along here don't bother, you know. They say it's too expensive.' She shivered, pulling the blanket around her shoulders. 'Bet they'll change their minds now though.'

'What about passersby?' said Kay. 'Any trouble from those?'

Briony shrugged. 'We get the odd drunk now and again. Sometimes a group of lads will walk past after the pubs close. Rupert – he owns the cabin cruiser over there – is pretty good about reading them the riot act if they make too much noise though.'

'We'll be checking CCTV as a routine part of our investigation. Did you hear anything before your boat caught fire?'

'No. I only woke up when I heard the window break and then the smoke alarm went off.'

Kay rose to her feet and ran her gaze over the destroyed home, a deadly calm returning to the riverbank now that the fire had been subdued. 'Do you have someone to help you with this?'

'I'm insured.' Briony sniffed. 'It doesn't make

up for the heirlooms and everything of course, but I'm glad I renewed it last week. Ellie's already been on the phone to them and they're sending out a salvage team with the assessor in the morning.'

Christie fished a business card from his pocket and passed it to her. 'We'll be in touch when we have an update, but if you think of anything that might help with our enquiries…'

Briony nodded. 'I will.'

He set a brisk pace back to the station, cutting through a short alleyway to a residential street running alongside the river, and Kay hurried to keep up.

When they reached the high street, he stopped suddenly and turned to her.

'You shouldn't do that.'

'What?'

'Make promises like you did back there. Telling victims you're going to find out who wronged them.' Christie took off as the pedestrian lights blinked green, slowing until she caught up. 'It doesn't always work out that way.'

'I know, but if I don't believe that, then what's the point?'

Her colleague led the way around the corner to the police station, swiped his security card and held open the door for her. 'Just remember you said that when we have to phone her to say that we've got no new leads and suspects.'

Kay watched as he took the stairs two at a time, and exhaled slowly.

'Then we just don't let that happen, do we?' she muttered.

FOUR

Kay dragged a spare chair with a broken wheel across the incident room, trying to ignore the pitiful squeaks from the other casters.

A small group was gathering around Detective Sergeant Devon Sharp, who in turn paced before a whiteboard strewn with coloured ink.

'Right, settle down and we'll make a start. For those of you who don't know me, I've been assigned SIO to a consolidated investigation into three suspicious fires in the area involving two narrowboats and a cabin cruiser. DC Richard Christie will deputise for me if I'm not around. Get to know each other after the briefing – we've got a lot to cover.'

Kay wriggled in her chair to offset the lack of seat padding and then craned her neck to see over the heads of two tall constables as the DS beckoned to a thin man in his mid-twenties who stood ramrod straight beside the board.

'Before we start, I'd like to introduce you to

DC Blake Travis. He qualified six months ago and will be here to gain some more experience until HQ assign him to a permanent role. Kay, I'd like you to ensure he can find everything he needs while he settles in. I'm sure you'll all make him welcome.'

Travis cleared his throat. 'Thanks, Sarge. I hope to make a significant contribution to this investigation given current staffing capabilities.'

He aimed a smug look at Kay with his last words, a smirk twitching the corner of his mouth.

She felt her jaw drop, then clamped it shut as Sharp continued.

'Right, note that we're only looking at these three fires – there was another one eight weeks ago, but that has been confirmed as being caused by an electrical fault so don't let that one distract you.' The DS rapped his knuckles against the whiteboard. 'The first fire happened on a narrowboat moored down near Haysden Country Park. The owner – Jared White – says he heard glass breaking, and then the galley went up in smoke. He only got out because he smashed a chair through the window of his cabin. The fire investigator's report confirms a small petrol bomb was used, exactly the same as this morning's incident.'

Kay's pen flew across her notebook as she kept up with Sharp's commentary, her thoughts racing.

'The second arson attack took place on the other side of town, just north of Tudeley Hale, and the outcome wasn't pleasant.' The DS pointed to four photographs that showed a twisted melted hull and not much else. 'Sam Donaldson was a retired army captain with two children. Luckily they weren't on board when this happened because they live with their mother during the week, but Sam didn't stand a chance. By the time the fire crew got to him, he'd succumbed to smoke inhalation and had third degree burns.'

Sharp turned back to the group. 'Kay, I'd like you to identify the witness statements from the first two fires and re-interview those people while uniformed officers finish the house-to-house enquiries from this morning's incident. We need to establish whether there's a connection between the three arson victims or whether the person who's doing this is picking boats at random. Work with Travis on this one – I'll need Christie working through this morning's statements as they come in.'

'Will do, Sarge.'

Travis rolled his eyes, then lowered his head to his notebook before Sharp could see.

Kay bit back a sigh and continued to listen as the DS worked his way around the circle of gathered officers, issuing tasks and giving advice before dismissing them.

Christie caught up with her as the team dispersed to their desks, and grinned.

'Watch out, Hunter. Looks like our new arrival might have his eye on your job here.'

She smiled sweetly at Travis as he walked past, then glared at Christie.

'Not a chance in hell.'

FIVE

'I take it that you doing this means Christie's on the fast track to a promotion then, not you?'

Kay wrenched the handbrake, plucked the keys from the ignition and then glared across at Travis, who stared through the windscreen, a perpetual twist to his mouth.

'Speaking to these people might shed some light on what happened this morning,' she said patiently. 'It could be important.'

'Could be…'

He gave a slight shake of his head and opened the door, sending a gust of wind into the car that sent discarded fast food wrappers and receipts swirling in a maelstrom across the back seat.

Kay climbed out, aimed the key fob over her shoulder and followed him across a boggy path that cut through the swollen meadow leading down to the river's edge.

During the summer, this place would be

teeming with families, walking groups and avid birdwatchers but the only people she could see today were a pair of cyclists on a path in the distance, heads bowed against a ferocious headwind.

'Who are we meeting?' Travis slowed so she could catch up, his slim frame huddled within a sleek woollen coat. 'There are four boats moored along here.'

Kay pulled her flimsy anorak around her chest and shivered. 'Didn't you read the witness statements?'

'You were, so I didn't see the point. No sense in doubling up. I was reading the victims' statements instead. Quite shocking they were, too.'

'Right…' Kay eyed him sideways, then led the way across to the moorings. 'Well, first up is Neville Warwick. His boat is that large cabin cruiser on the end, *The Lancaster*.'

'Okay. What did he have to say for himself?'

'If you'd read the statements like Sharp told us to…'

Travis flapped his hand with annoyance. 'Just give me the headlines, all right?'

She paused a few metres away from the boat and lowered her voice. 'Neville was night fishing at the lake – not in the rule book, mind, so the anglers' association have banned him from doing that again – and on the way back here he says he saw someone running away from the moorings. Obviously, it was dark so he lost sight of whoever it was and was unable to give us a description apart from dark clothing and what could either be close-cropped hair or a beanie hat. Jared's boat went up in flames a couple of minutes later. If it wasn't for Jared smashing the window and Neville risking his own life to pull him out, we'd have another murder on our hands.'

Travis whistled under his breath, then peered over her shoulder at the sound of the cabin cruiser's door swinging open. 'This must be him. Shall I lead, and you can take notes?'

'I—'

But he was already striding across to the boat owner, hand outstretched. 'Neville Warwick? Detective Constable Blake Travis. I'm assisting DS Devon Sharp with the arson enquiry. I wondered if I could have a quick word.'

Kay trudged forwards, pulling her notebook from her bag as Travis stepped over the gunwale at Warwick's invitation and took a seat on the wraparound sofa that hugged the back deck.

'Detective Constable Kay Hunter,' she mumbled, nodding her thanks as the owner reached out and took her hand to guide her over.

'Is this about the fire yesterday?' he said, reaching into the top pocket of a worn denim jacket and extracting a pack of cigarettes. 'Heard someone else's boat went up in smoke. Lucky to get out, wasn't she?'

'She was indeed, Mr Warwick.' Travis cast his gaze about the river while the man lit up. 'Nice spot here.'

'Bit quieter now after the fire. It put a few of them off, and it's not tourist season yet.'

Travis swung round to face him again. 'Do you like the peace and quiet, Mr Warwick?'

The man's eyes narrowed. 'What are you implying?'

'Nothing at all.' Travis smiled, but Kay noticed it didn't reach his eyes. 'Your statement says you were returning from night fishing when Jared's boat caught fire. What time was that?'

'About two, I suppose.'

'Catch much?'

'Couple of decent sized bream.'

'Did anyone see you?'

'No, not unless whoever set fire to Jared's boat spotted me. Might be why they ran off.' Warwick tilted his head back and blew smoke into the air. 'Either that or they knew the damn thing was about to go up.'

Kay noticed the man shiver. 'Had you received any threats before the attack on your neighbour's boat?'

'There was a spate of vandalism and stuff going on for a bit. That petered out a couple of weeks before the fire. Apart from that, we're pretty much left alone here. Summer can be different but that's just normally people larking about, nothing serious.'

'Going back to the night in question,' said Travis, pausing to aim a pointed stare at Kay. 'Could you smell anything when you got closer to your neighbour's boat? Petrol, perhaps?'

Warwick frowned. 'Maybe, yes. I mean, something had to have been used to make it go up like that. Either fuel or gas, right?'

'How long was it between you getting back here and the boat catching fire?'

'No more than a couple of minutes. I lost sight of whoever it was running away, and was looking over there towards the cycle path in case they used that, but then there was this almighty sound like a clap of thunder and the front two windows of Jared's boat exploded outwards.' Warwick flicked his spent cigarette into the water, ignoring Kay's protest. 'After that, I was too busy trying to get him out of there, then moving this one so she didn't catch fire as well.'

He coughed, then turned at the sound of another man's voice.

Kay looked over her shoulder to see a man in his thirties approaching, his grey suit trousers flecked with mud and water as he traipsed across the meadow towards them.

'That'll be the bloke from the insurance company, so you'll have to push off. Jared recommended him 'cause they're paying out on his without a fight. With another fire yesterday, I figured I'd be an idiot not to.'

Travis rose to his feet. 'Thanks for your time, Mr Warwick. If you think of anything else, could you get in touch with DS Sharp?'

'That I will.'

Kay slipped her notebook away, climbed over

the gunwale and walked over to intercept the insurance broker.

'Morning,' she said.

'Are you the police?'

'Routine questions, that's all.' Travis elbowed his way past her and stuck out his hand, introducing himself. 'You are...?'

'Cameron Usher. I've got a meeting with Mr Warwick at ten.' He handed Travis a business card.

'Selling insurance, eh?'

The man gave a slight shrug. 'Someone has to, right?'

'Doesn't Mr Warwick already have insurance?'

'No.' Usher waved his hand in the direction of the river. 'A lot of the people who live along here don't bother with anything other than the basic cover, thinking it's cheaper. Or they only insure for their contents, forgetting if their vessel is damaged or destroyed, often it's their homes and livelihood that goes with it.'

'Seen much business this way?'

'I've seen an increase these past few weeks, yes. What with the recent spate of vandalism and arson attacks, and nobody claiming responsibility.' Usher sighed. 'I just wish I could convince the others.'

'Right, well, we'll let you get on.'

Travis set out for the parked car, swinging his arms as Kay stumbled to keep up. 'That went well, didn't it? Plenty to think about there.'

'Uh-huh.'

'Who's next on the list then, Hunter?' He

walked around to the passenger side of the car. 'You might as well drive to the next place too. I can give Sharp an update on the way. Might as well keep up the momentum, don't you think?'

'Whatever you say,' Kay muttered and threw her bag on the back seat.

SIX

The sun was attempting an appearance by the time Kay had driven through Tonbridge and out the other side.

She flipped down the windscreen visor before taking a narrow winding lane towards Tudeley Hale, slowing when she reached the village.

Passing a gastropub on the right, she realised it had been weeks since she had had the time to treat herself, and a smile formed on her lips as she recalled someone at the station recommending the place.

Her thoughts turned back to the investigation at the sound of a grunt from the passenger seat.

She and Travis hadn't spoken since she'd accelerated away from the country park, gritting her teeth as she listened to him informing Sharp that his interview with Neville Warwick had gone well, and that – at his suggestion no less – they were now heading towards the moorings at Porter's Lock.

He coughed. 'Who are we—'

'Meeting? The witness who phoned triple nine when Sam's boat caught fire, Michelle Chereton,' said Kay, exasperated. 'Really, you should've at least skim-read these statements to learn what's been going on.'

'I don't need to, you have. Like I said, no sense in doubling up.'

'Fine, but I'd like to lead this interview. There are a couple of questions I've got for Michelle relating to a report she filed two months ago concerning vandalism that hasn't been followed up yet.'

'Such as?'

Kay shifted down a gear, the sign for the lock flashing past Travis's window. 'Both she and Sam had windows broken, but a week after that, Sam's boat was sprayed with graffiti – hers wasn't. I'm wondering why.'

'You think someone was singling out Sam and leaving Michelle alone?'

'Maybe. I don't know yet. That's what I'd like to find out.'

'Okay, sounds like a plan.'

She relaxed then, pulling into a small gravel car park signposted for the residents of the moorings only, and running through the forthcoming interview in her mind.

Leading the way through a wooden kissing gate that separated the car park from the towpath, she spotted Michelle's brightly painted boat,

Summer Breeze at the far end of a line of three moorings.

The first two boats she passed were deserted, almost sinking under the amount of mould and algae that clung to the hulls. She curled her lip at the smell of decay coming from them and wondered how long they'd been abandoned.

'What a dump,' Travis said, brushing past her as she paused to take a photo on her phone. 'Why anyone would want to live on a boat is beyond me.'

'It's freedom, I suppose,' said Kay. 'And the scenery always changes.'

He mumbled something under his breath, then turned at movement from Michelle's boat. 'Ah, there she is. Ms Chereton? Detective Constable Blake Travis. Got a minute to have a chat?'

Kay shook her head as he hurried towards the woman. 'Bloody cheeky bastard. He's done it again…'

By the time she caught up with him, he was chatting to Michelle amiably, admiring the small collection of potted herbs that covered the roof of her narrowboat and cooing over the fairy lights that dangled around the tiny deck.

'This is my colleague, DC Hunter,' he said as she approached. 'If you're ready, Kay, shall we make a start?'

'Ready whenever you are.' Kay already had her notebook out, choosing to stand on the towpath rather than risk squeezing onto the deck with Travis.

She might accidentally push him into the river.

'What can you tell me about the night of the fire?' Travis crossed his legs, leaning back on the plush cushions and looking for all the world like he belonged there.

'I gave a statement at the time,' said Michelle.

'Humour me. I'd like to hear it in your own words.'

'Oh. Well, I suppose it was about half-past ten when I heard a noise. At first, I didn't know what it was, but then I could smell smoke. When I opened the door, I could see flames... I keep a fire extinguisher here so I grabbed that and ran, but I couldn't get close enough to use it.' She paused and wiped her eyes. 'I could hear him inside, screaming and coughing but I...'

Kay swallowed, waiting for Travis to offer some words of comfort.

None came.

'And where was Sam's boat in relation to yours?' He twisted in his seat. 'I can't see any damage to yours.'

'He was moored at the other end, past these two.'

'In your statement, you said that your windows were broken in the weeks leading up to it,' said Travis. 'Were you being harassed at all before that?'

Kay's pen went through the thin paper, and she turned the page, swearing under her breath.

'Sam reported it at the time, actually, and someone came out to take a look,' said Michelle. She leaned against the cabin door while she stared at the deck. 'We were already patching up the windows by then the best we could, but it took forever to get all the glass out of the reeds around here. I was worried the ducks might tread on it.'

'And no-one claimed responsibility?'

Michelle straightened, then arched an eyebrow. 'Not to my knowledge. Have they?'

Kay bit back a snort at Travis's face, and instead raised her voice. 'Are you all right out here, on your own? I mean, these two boats look abandoned, and…'

'I'm okay.' Michelle gave a shrug. 'Morris who owns the boatyard down the road has been brilliant, really. When the windows were smashed, he did us a deal for both boats to save us some money, and then when Sam's boat was vandalised again, he came down here with all the paint and helped him clean it up.' She tugged at a thread at the wrist of her thick woollen cardigan. 'He's been a godsend, especially since… since the fire.'

'How did—'

'Didn't your insurers pay for the windows to be replaced?' Travis said, ignoring the glare Kay aimed his way. 'I mean, it can't be cheap – these are specialist sizes, aren't they?'

'They are, and neither of us was insured at the time.'

'At the time?'

Michelle nodded. 'After what happened to Sam, I phoned up the broker who came to see us a week or so before the fire and told him I wanted to take out a policy straight away. I can't afford to lose my home.'

Kay heard Travis's sharp intake of breath as he leaned forward.

'What was the broker's name?' he said.

SEVEN

Kay sat staring at her computer screen, chin in her hand while she scrolled through the additional notes she had added to the HOLMES2 database upon her return to the incident room.

Across the room, she could hear Christie's familiar laugh as he joked with PC Lisa Nash and her colleague before the two uniformed constables said their farewells and headed out to start another shift.

He wandered past on the way back to his desk, took one look at Kay's face, and dropped into the seat beside her.

'That bad, eh?'

'That bad.'

His attention turned to her screen. 'How did you get on this morning?'

'We spoke to a couple of witnesses who were there at the time of the fires, but who also experienced vandalism to their boats at the same time as the victims of the fires.' She leaned back and rubbed at tired eyes. 'I'm wondering whether there's a connection but I can't see it yet, and all the time Sharp has me teamed up with Travis, I'm not going to get a word in edgeways. I mean, it's bad enough that he's taking credit for my suggestions – I can live with that if it gets us a result – but his communication skills are…'

'Requiring some practice?' Christie smiled, then, seeing Travis heading their way, rose from his chair and patted her on the shoulder. 'Hang in there.'

'Yeah.'

'Richard,' Travis bellowed as he dropped his wallet and phone beside his computer keyboard. 'Any luck at your end, or still chasing leads?'

'Working on it,' replied Christie, and shot a wink at Kay before walking away.

'Well.' Travis smacked his hands together, then shot back his cuffs and logged in. 'Did you put the updates in the system, Kay?'

'I have.'

'Good stuff. Got to admit, I hate all the admin stuff. Much better when one team member takes responsibility for it all, don't you think?'

Kay bit down hard on the inside of her cheek and clicked "save". 'I think we need to widen the scope of our enquiry.'

'Oh? In what way?'

'These vandalism claims. Every one of the arson victims had their boats vandalised before the fires.'

'Weeks before the fires. There's no connection.'

'Yes, but…' She looked up as DS Sharp strode towards them.

'How are you getting on with the witnesses?' he said.

Kay straightened in her seat. 'Sarge, I think that—'

'Kay thinks that we should widen the parameters,' said Travis, cutting her off and raising his voice. 'Personally, I feel that the insurance broker, Cameron Usher, has a motive. After all, he makes more money in commission the more owners that sign up to the policies on offer. I read Briony Peters' statement last night before leaving the station, and she said that many of the owners have been reluctant to sign up because it's so expensive. They're changing their minds in droves now. There's a real sense of fear in the community because of the fires.'

Kay dug her fingernails into her palms and kept her gaze firmly on her computer screen, her jaw clenched.

'It's a very good point,' Sharp said. 'And it's certainly worth following up in the morning. What were you going to say, Kay?'

'Travis has got a fair point about the broker,' she conceded. 'But Michelle Chereton, Briony Peters and Neville Warwick told us that before the fires, there were vandalism incidents, and not all of those were reported to the police. They might have a point – so far, none of the attacks have targeted tourists, only locals. I'd like to take a look into it.'

'Waste of time,' Travis brayed. 'It's a huge step from breaking a few windows to petrol bombing someone's home.'

'But I think that—'

'Kay, if you want to follow that line of enquiry, do so. Travis, you follow up about the broker. Kay can help you with that, given you're not familiar with the area yet.' Sharp turned away. 'I'll leave you both to get on with it, but you know where I am if you need me.'

Kay watched him go, then turned back to see Travis staring at her. 'What?'

'You can look into the vandalism on your own,' he said. 'I'm not watching my career going up in smoke chasing a bad lead.'

She pushed back her chair and squared her shoulders, picked up her coffee cup and then leaned down to murmur in his ear as she passed him.

'You don't *have* a career yet, Travis.'

EIGHT

Kay chose to walk to Ellie Greening's house to interview Briony Peters rather than take one of the pool cars.

As she waited at the pedestrian crossing on Tonbridge High Street, the fresh nip to the air softened her temper and blew away some of the frustration and antipathy she was feeling towards Blake Travis.

She wondered whether his arrogance came from a deep-seated lack of confidence in his abilities, and then the crossing signal zapped and she recalled his laziness and reluctance to learn about the previous fires.

Shoving her hands into her pockets, she resolved to follow the lead she had suggested to Sharp, figuring that the DS wouldn't have agreed to let her pursue it if he didn't think it worthwhile.

Walking down a side street towards the boat moorings, she turned her focus to her own investigation, and the questions she wanted to ask Briony Peters.

After pausing to check her notes, she knocked on the door of an end of terrace backing onto the river and took a step back as a figure appeared behind the frosted glass panelling.

Ellie Greening's brow furrowed when she opened the door. 'Any news?'

'Actually, I was wondering if Briony was in and whether I could ask her a few more questions.'

'She's in the living room, come on through.'

Kay followed her through a door off to the left of a narrow hallway and found herself in a comfortable space with French windows looking out to a short tidy garden. Over the back of a wooden panelled fence, she could see the playing fields beyond the river, the watercourse hidden by a line of bamboo that Ellie had planted at some point.

'Hello, Detective Hunter.' Briony uncurled herself from a large armchair, balancing a coffee mug between her hands. 'I take it there's been no progress yet.'

'We're following up some leads at the present time, but I'm afraid that's all I can say at the moment. Would you mind if I asked you some more questions?'

'Have a seat,' said Ellie, gesturing to the sofa.

Kay eyed the cat that was glaring at her from its position on one of the sofa's arms and chose a spot at the opposite end.

The cat raised its tail and sprang to the floor.

'How are you getting on, Briony?' Kay said. 'Is there anything you need?'

The woman shook her head. 'Thanks for asking, but no. Ellie's done more than enough for me, and I've already spoken to my insurers. Given the police are treating this as arson, not an accident, they don't think it'll take long for them to send me some money until the claim's processed in full.'

'That's good to hear.'

Briony's face suddenly turned stricken at the sound of a ripping noise. 'Oi, stop that!'

Kay looked down in time to see Briony's cat release its claws from the side of Ellie's sofa before it scarpered upstairs.

'God, I'm sorry, El. He's just not used to being cooped up.' Briony sighed, exasperated. 'Talk about being ungrateful.'

The other woman waved the apology away. 'It's an old sofa, and we'll get him a scratching post this afternoon.'

Kay bit back a smile, knowing the cat would probably ignore the new toy and take to carving up one of the other chairs instead before long. 'Briony, I realise this will sound like I'm asking you to repeat yourself, but it may be that you recall something today that you might've overlooked on Monday.'

'I wouldn't be surprised,' said Briony stoically. 'I've been thinking a lot about who might've done this to me, but I don't think I've annoyed anyone and I get on fine with my ex-husband now that we're living apart. Anyway, he was in Edinburgh these past four days for a conference so…'

'I'd like to go back to the vandalism you said you and some other boat owners experienced. What happened there?'

Briony cradled her mug in her hands and leaned back against the sofa cushions. 'It felt like harassment the first time – you know, kids causing trouble. But by the second time, I wasn't the only one starting to get nervous. Rupert – the man with the cabin cruiser I told you about – got his insurance broker over because he was worried a few of us didn't have enough cover, and we lodged another report with the police.'

Kay's stomach flipped at the mention of the broker. 'Can you remember the insurance bloke's name?'

'Cameron someone-or-other. Rupert'll have his card.'

'That's okay. Thanks. Again, I can only apologise that you felt your reports weren't taken seriously at the time.' Kay lowered her gaze and pondered her next question before asking, 'What changed between the second and third vandalism attacks?'

'It seemed more targeted,' said Briony. 'The people who could afford insurance took it out, knowing that if anything more serious happened, they'd have enough of a payout to at least go to the boatyard along from here safe in the knowledge they could afford a replacement home and that all their contents were insured. We'd heard about the two fires then, and although the police weren't saying it, we couldn't help feeling that they were connected somehow. Then, when the third bout of windows being smashed happened, it was to boats like mine. Owners who hadn't taken out the new insurance policies.'

'Can I ask why you didn't?'

Briony dabbed at her eyes with the sleeve of her sweatshirt. 'I couldn't afford to. I'll get something for the boat with the policy I've got, and all my contents were insured, but I'll have to downsize. I don't want to get a mortgage at my age, you see – the banks won't lend to me anyway without a fight, because I'm self-employed. I've already had a chat with Morris at the boatyard about getting something secondhand through him,' she said, forcing a smile. 'I realised I don't need anything as big as I had, now that my grown-up kids don't visit so much, and he says he can do me a deal.'

'Is that the one along from here?' Kay asked.

'No, and Morris's yard isn't as big,' explained Ellie, 'but he's relatively new compared to them, and seems to make an effort for all the locals. I'm sure he'll have Briony back on her feet in no time.'

'What's the name of the yard?'

'Dagenham Chandlers. It's on the other side of town. Halfway between here and Porter's Lock.' Briony held up crossed fingers. 'I just have to hope the insurers pay out otherwise Ellie's going to get fed up with me taking up space.'

'Not at all.' Her friend grimaced. 'Though if you don't mind me saying, I don't think I'll miss your cat.'

NINE

Kay parked the pool car beside a pockmarked blue steel gate held open with a piece of thick rope, and shrugged her coat around her shoulders as she walked into the chandler's yard.

To her right, closest to the river and taking up most of the space on the expansive concrete hardstanding were eight small- to medium-sized cabin cruisers and motorboats. Each had a printed sign fixed to its prow displaying the prices, and she realised that they were all secondhand rather than the new boats that jostled for space at the larger marina in Tonbridge.

On her left was a clutch of shipping containers in various colours, well worn with rust and chipped paint hanging off their sides, and it was next to the farthest one that she spotted a man in dark blue overalls, head bowed while he applied an angle grinder to a chunky metal rod.

Not wishing to be blinded by the sparks, she

waited off to the side until the man moved and caught sight of her.

Immediately, the rod flickered out, and he raised his protective faceguard. 'Help you?'

Kay raised her warrant card. 'DC Hunter, Kent Police. Are you Morris Dagenham?'

'I am.' He paused to wipe grease-smeared hands with an even greasier rag and dropped the faceguard onto the workbench beside him. 'This about the fires?'

'And the vandalism before those.'

'Terrible business.' He gave a slight shake of his head, then beckoned to her. 'Come on in. It's warmer in the office – Louise, my wife, is here doing the book-keeping this morning so she'll have the heater going full blast knowing her.'

He wasn't wrong.

When Kay followed him into the cavernous workshop, eyeing the enormous fibreglass hull that took up most of the space, and then through to a box-like office sequestered at the back of the building, she was hit by a blast of hot air that was reminiscent of the heat emanating from the welding torch.

Morris slammed shut the door as soon as she entered. 'Best to keep it in, otherwise the costs'll go through the roof. Lou, this is Detective Hunter. She wanted to talk to us about the fires and all that.'

Kay turned her attention to the woman behind a chipped Formica table that served as the single desk in the cramped space while he moved towards an electric heater in the corner, turning down the dial before straightening.

The woman twisted her hair into a top knot, stuck a pencil through it and held out her hand. 'Louise Dagenham. Do you want a cuppa?'

'I wouldn't normally accept, but…'

'It's bloody cold, and we're having one, so don't worry about formalities for goodness sakes.' Louise was already moving towards a kettle, made small talk while it boiled, and then handed Kay a steaming mug of strong tea. 'I've put a splash of cold in it so you can drink it straight away.'

'Thanks.' Kay warmed her hands around it, her watch catching the light from a large window that took up one side of the office and looked out over the River Medway below. 'I'll bet this place is beautiful in the summer.'

'It is,' said Morris, indicating two chairs in front of the desk and sinking into one of them. 'And busy out there. Always something to look at.'

'As if you have time for that.' Louise smiled indulgently, before turning her attention to Kay. 'He's always in the workshop doing something.'

'Boats are like that, aren't they? They always need something doing to them.' Kay sipped her tea. 'I remember that from canal holidays when I was a kid.'

'Happier times?' Morris asked, noticing her reticence.

'Yeah. I don't see much of my parents these days.' Kay put down the mug. 'Anyway, sorry – I'm meant to be asking you some questions about our investigation into recent arson attacks on boat owners, as well as the murder of one of them. I understand Jared White has ordered a replacement boat from you recently?'

'God, he was so lucky his insurers paid out,' said Louise. 'Did you know we helped out Sam Donaldson after his and Michelle Chereton's boats had their windows smashed as well? The sooner you find out whoever's doing this, the better. Do you think we're safe here, in the yard?'

Her gaze travelled to the dirt-stained glass, her brow furrowing as she peered out.

'At present, I don't think you need to worry,' said Kay, 'but out of interest, what security measures do you have here?'

'The gate's locked after five o'clock at night, and that wire fence is high enough to keep out most would-be burglars. The workshop locks were changed about a year or so ago after one of them failed. We figured we might as well get the inner office one changed and the storage sheds at the same time while we had the locksmith here.' Louise turned and pointed at the computer on the corner of her husband's desk. 'And Morris set up CCTV cameras six months ago – he can view the playback here or on the laptop at home.'

'Good, okay – back to the arson attacks. Any idea who might be targeting boat owners along here? I mean, you run a busy chandlers business out of here, so I imagine you hear all sorts of things from people passing through.'

'I haven't heard anything,' said Morris.

'Although I can assure you, I'm keeping my ears open.'

Louise shot her a sardonic smile. 'You're right, people do like to gossip. So far, from what I gather, most people think it's teenagers because of the vandalism to the windows. It's the sort of thing kids do, right?'

'I sense a "but"…'

'I just can't see teenagers going as far as putting a petrol bomb through someone's window, can you? I mean, Jared said that's what was used to set his boat on fire. It's more vindictive, isn't it? Breaking windows or graffitiing someone's boat is nasty, but setting fire to someone's home? I just don't understand it.' The woman shivered despite the heat belching out from the electric fire. 'That's what scares me. If someone did get into the yard and put a petrol bomb through one of these windows, we'd lose the whole lot, just like Jared.'

'How sure are you that it was kids who vandalised the boats along from here?'

Louise shot her husband a sideways glance. 'Well, because Morris caught one of them.'

'Really?' Kay flicked through her notes. 'It's just that his neighbour didn't mention that.'

'If Sam didn't tell Michelle, there's no reason why she'd have known,' said Morris. 'When Sam told me the day after he found the graffiti what had happened to his boat, I came back here to check the recordings. Sure enough, I spotted the little bugger walking back to the boat his parents had hired on my CCTV cameras. He dumped the empty spray cans in a skip round the back of the workshop here. So me and Sam went over to the tourist moorings to have a word.' He grinned. 'I reckon the little sod's ears were ringing all the way back home.'

'What about the windows that were smashed before that? Was that the same kid?'

'No, we never found out who that was,' said Louise. 'There weren't any tourist boats around then. As it was, that particular family were only down this way on holiday because they couldn't fly to Lanzarote as planned – the kid's sister broke her leg the week before so the narrowboat holiday was plan B for them.'

'And the pair of them were miserable as anything,' Morris added, shaking his head. 'I'd have loved to have done something like that when I was their age.'

Kay snapped shut her notebook. 'I think that's all the questions I've got for now, but here's my card in case you think of anything else.'

'Let us know if we can help with anything, won't you?' said Morris. 'I know it'll sound selfish given Sam lost his life only a few weeks ago, but I can't help worrying what'll happen if whoever's behind all this turns their attention to this place.'

Louise slipped her arm around him. 'Don't worry, love. It's boats that are being targeted, not boatyards.'

'I'll give you a call as soon as I've got something to share,' said Kay. 'Thanks for your time.'

She walked back to the car, tossed her bag onto the back seat and then rummaged in her pocket as her phone vibrated.

When she read the text message from Christie, her heart sank.

Blake Travis had made an arrest.

TEN

Kay took the stairs up to the incident room two at a time, nearly colliding with Christie on the landing as he emerged from the third-floor door.

'Woah, steady.' He held up a hand. 'Got my message, then?'

'What happened? Where is he? Who—'

Christie wrapped his hand around her arm and led her back down a flight of stairs. 'Calm down. They're doing the interview at the moment.'

'Who is?'

Her colleague paused at the next landing, his gaze travelling to his shoes. 'Travis and Sharp.'

'Oh, for f——'

Kay spun away from him, staring out the window that overlooked the rooftops along a cluster of side streets beyond the main thoroughfare. Her eyes stung, and her heart rammed against her ribs as she fought back anger, frustration…

'Come on. Let's go and find a quiet place to have a coffee.'

Christie gave her a gentle nudge, so she followed him out of the police station and along to a cafe that was almost deserted after the lunchtime trade had ended.

'We're closing in half an hour,' said the burly woman behind the counter as she swept away crumbs from the cake displays. 'And we stopped serving food an hour ago.'

'We're just after two coffees.' Christie paid and carried the drinks over to a table at the back of the cafe. 'Sit.'

Kay did as she was told, plucked two sugar sachets from a pot on the table and dumped the contents into her drink. 'What happened?'

'Travis interviewed Cameron Usher late last night, and apparently wasn't satisfied with the answers he got, so he went to see his manager this morning and it transpires Usher's been bringing in more work than usual lately.'

'What does that mean?' Kay took a sip of the coffee and winced as the hot liquid scorched her lips.

'Usher and his colleagues work on a commission basis, so they earn a basic salary – very basic in the case of this particular brokerage – and are expected to sign up a certain number of clients every month in order to earn more and meet their targets.'

'And I take it Usher's meeting those targets?'

'Not just meeting them – exceeding them. By a

long way. His manager was really impressed with him until Travis turned up.'

'How many boat owners has he signed up since the fires then?'

'Twenty-nine.'

Kay's jaw dropped. 'All from Tonbridge?'

'No, some are from further afield, like Maidstone, but you know how word spreads in communities like that. People are scared.'

'What about alibis?'

'Brokers work alone, remotely from the office,' said Christie. 'He only has to check in once or twice a week and as long as he keeps in touch via phone or email, he and his colleagues are left alone to sign up business wherever they can. It's pretty cutthroat out there at the moment, too, from what Usher's manager told Travis. Everyone at the brokerage is worried about losing their job, and potential customers don't want to pay out for the cover because they can't afford it.'

'So Usher's been forcing the issue by vandalising boats, and when that hasn't worked he's petrol-bombed them.' Kay leaned back in her seat. 'Looks like Travis is onto something then.'

'Don't be disappointed you didn't get the breakthrough,' Christie said gently. 'Just be glad we can put a stop to the arson attacks before somebody else is killed.'

'I know.' Kay ran a hand through her hair, then smiled. 'Well, while we're out of earshot of everyone in the station, have you proposed to Sadie yet?'

'It's bedlam at home at the moment. One of the kids is off sick from school with a streaming cold, I'm working all hours on this case at the moment...'

'Excuses, excuses.'

'Yeah, I know.' He sighed. 'I'll ask her, don't worry.'

Kay looked down as her phone pinged with a message and fished it from her bag, her smile widening

'Is that the vet?'

Her head snapped up, heat flushing her cheeks. 'Who told you about him?'

Christie grinned. 'Might've heard something from Lisa in passing.'

Kay shook her head, unable to hide a smile. She would have a word with the uniformed constable the next time she saw her.

'Well, is it serious?'

'Maybe. I don't know yet.'

Her colleague cocked his head to one side while he watched her text a reply. 'You met him at Christmas didn't you?'

'Yes.' She tucked her phone away. 'It's just that...'

'What?'

'I don't know – we're both so busy. Him with trying to keep up with work and his studies, me doing this...'

'If it's meant to be, it'll work out. Look at me and Sadie. She works all hours at the hospital, but we manage.'

'True. Except for that marriage proposal thing.'

'Stop changing the subject.' Christie laughed, drained his coffee and stood. 'Come on. Plenty of paperwork to get through this afternoon, even if you're not leading the suspect interview.'

ELEVEN

The next day, Kay had arrived at work to discover that Cameron Usher had been retained in custody and that DS Sharp had applied to hold him for another twelve hours.

The questioning had gone on for most of the day but with four hours of their extended timeline remaining, rumours were swirling around the incident room that charges would be laid before long.

Now, with sodium streetlights casting a soft hue through the plastic blinds at the windows, she sat with her back to the darkened view over Tonbridge, scrolling through the statements she had processed.

After scribbling a note to remind herself to double-check when Michelle Chereton had taken out her insurance policy, she dropped her pen and looked up as Travis approached.

He bounced rather than walked towards her,

grinning widely and smacking his hands together when he reached her desk.

'Well, Hunter, looks like that's one-nil to me, eh?' he said, loosening his tie. 'Are you going to buy me a drink to celebrate after we charge him?'

She crossed her arms over her chest. 'In case you missed it, someone died because of one of these fires, Travis. Two people lost their homes, and their neighbours were bloody lucky they didn't lose theirs too.'

He sobered immediately. 'Well, I… of course, of course.'

'It's not about win or lose, Travis. I do this job because I care about the people I help. Not about your point-scoring.'

'What about that drink?'

'I don't think so, do you?'

She picked up her pen once more and ignored him until he slunk away, and wondered for a fleeting moment whether he would perhaps think on her words and what responsibilities lay ahead in his role.

Then she heard his braying voice and Lisa Nash laughing with him and groaned as, one by one, her colleagues followed him out of the room.

An hour later, a piping hot Chinese takeaway to one side and a soft drink in her hand, she pored over the witness statements that she had printed out and laid across her desk.

She had spent the past two hours watching the recordings of Cameron Usher's interview with Travis and Sharp, the man becoming more agitated as the day progressed, in turn pleading with them to believe him and then refusing to disclose where he had been when fires happened.

And yet, something still niggled her.

Her phone vibrated across the desk and she snatched it up, her heart sinking as she read the new message.

Fancy a drink tonight? x

'Dammit.' She typed out a reply. *Can't, still working. Sorry x*

Exhaling, she flipped through another statement, lost in the words as she tried to piece together the missing information in Cameron Usher's answers.

'Care to share?'

She spun around at the sound of Sharp's voice to see the DS leaning against Christie's, his grey eyes full of worry.

'Sorry, Sarge – didn't see you there.'

He moved closer, and she held out the bag of complimentary prawn crackers.

'Don't tell anyone, I'm supposed to be on a diet and Rebecca will kill me if she finds out.'

Despite everything, Kay smiled. She had met the DS's wife once or twice at social events and had instantly built up a rapport with the woman. 'Your secret's safe with me, Sarge.'

'So,' he said between mouthfuls. 'How did you get on yesterday? I never got the chance to catch up with you.'

'The graffiti to Sam Donaldson's boat was done by a teenager on holiday. The owner of the yard at Porter's Lock caught him on CCTV and he and Sam confronted the parents.'

'Not related to the windows being smashed along there then?'

'No. How's it going with Usher? Has he been charged yet?'

Sharp eyed her keenly. 'I've just advised Cameron Usher that he's no longer a person of interest in our investigation and that we're making arrangements to release him immediately.'

Her heart lurched.

'What happened? The way Travis was talking, it was a slam-dunk.'

The DS gave a weary smile.

'Travis may have thought he'd solved our case, but I'm afraid our latest recruit has got a steep learning curve ahead of him. Especially when it comes to doing his research properly before jumping to conclusions.'

'Oh?' Kay took a sip of soft drink. 'Why?'

'It turns out that Cameron Usher is Briony Peters' son. I just spoke with her. He's been running around trying to put together insurance deals for the local boat owners as a favour to her after she called him following the vandalism attacks.'

She snorted, sending bubbles up her nose and, spluttering, reached out for a paper handkerchief. 'Oh my god, sorry Sarge... I shouldn't laugh but... what about the celebratory drinks he organised?'

'I have a feeling he'll be drowning his sorrows instead.'

'Oh god…' She sobered. 'Why on earth didn't Cameron tell you all this in the first place?'

'He was worried it might shift blame onto his mother – apparently, she's been telling her neighbours for the past four months that she wants a new boat. He was scared that if he told us that, we might think she was responsible for the fires. As it is, Briony has solid alibis for every incident, and the fire investigation report has absolved her of any involvement in the one that destroyed her boat.'

'What a mess.'

'Indeed. Anyway – enjoy your dinner, Kay.' The DS leaned over, stealing another handful of the prawn crackers. 'And don't stay too late. I want to hear about the theory you've been working on first thing in the morning.'

'Thanks, Sarge. Will do.'

TWELVE

Kay rubbed at bleary eyes as she walked along Tonbridge High Street the next morning, her breath fogging in front of her.

Her alarm had gone off at five, and now she hurried towards the police station, determined to catch Sharp as soon as he arrived – and before Travis showed up.

Swiping her security card across the lock at reception, she raced up to the incident room, placed her bag under her desk, then took a moment to gather her thoughts.

She had spent the hours after Sharp left last night phoning witnesses, apologising for the late intrusion into their lives, and pulling together the final pieces of her theory until, exhausted, she had taken a taxi home, too tired to walk.

'Okay, Hunter. Make or break time,' she muttered.

Sweeping up copies of balance sheets obtained from the Companies House website, social media profiles and her notes, she crossed the room to Sharp's office.

The door was open, and as she neared she could see the DS's face illuminated by his computer screen, a stale aroma of coffee beans hanging in the air.

'Morning, Sarge. What time did you get in?'

He looked up at her voice and gestured to one of the chairs opposite his desk. 'About an hour ago.'

'It's only half six now, Sarge.'

'And what time did you leave last night?'

Kay bit her lip.

'Exactly. So, what have you got for me?'

She handed him the balance sheets. 'I think Travis was onto something when he went after Cameron Usher, but he just approached it at the wrong angle.'

Sharp raised an eyebrow. 'You're agreeing with Travis?'

'Not quite. I think if he'd been less concerned with getting a result, and more concerned with getting the right result, he might've come up with the same theory I have.'

'That's rather generous of you.'

'Perhaps.' She pointed at the documents in his hand. 'Morris and Louise Dagenham own a small boatyard near Porter's Lock. Until last year, they were doing okay – not making as much money as some of the bigger ones along the river, but enough to get by and live well on it.'

'What changed?'

'Morris was diagnosed with cancer nine months ago.'

'How did you find that out?'

Kay held up another page. 'Social media. His treatment was successful and he's currently in remission but it did mean that for six months, he couldn't take on any work other than basic repairs.' She leaned over and pointed at the last lines on the balance sheet. 'And their profits tumbled.'

'Go on.'

'Based on those figures and after chatting with Michelle Chereton who lives at Porter's Lock, I don't think the Dagenhams' business would have lasted much past this summer's tourist season. Except then, the vandalism started.'

'Minor repairs to tie them over the winter months, you mean?'

'That's what I'm thinking. Except there are only a finite number of boats moored along the river at this time of year, and if someone's windows are broken you're still in competition with other boatyards to do the repairs. Michelle said Morris Dagenham was the cheapest though, so she and Sam had their windows replaced by him. As did Jared and Briony.'

Sharp held up his hand. 'Wait a minute. Are you suggesting that the Dagenhams are behind these arson attacks and Sam Donaldson's murder?'

'Jared White put in an order for a new boat from them after his insurance claim was processed, and Briony Peters has said she's talking to them about a quote as well. The Dagenhams' yard provided cheaper quotes than its competitors, and probably on purpose so they can try to save the business.'

'How come you didn't ask them about all this when you interviewed them yesterday?'

'I didn't know about the boat sales, Sarge. Or the state of their accounts.'

Sharp lowered the balance sheets and stared at her. 'So if they're desperate for business, why kill Sam?'

'That's what I'd like to ask them, Sarge.'

'Get a warrant to search their premises and bring them both in for questioning, Kay.' His grey eyes sparkled. 'And you can lead the interviews with me this time.'

THIRTEEN

Morris Dagenham sat beside a harassed-looking duty solicitor and smoothed his thinning white hair across his scalp, sweat forming at his temples.

His oil-specked overalls had been replaced with a suit that hung from his slender frame, and his eyes shifted from Kay to Sharp as the DS started the recording equipment and recited the formal caution.

The duty solicitor uncapped her fountain pen and wrote the date and time at the top of her notepad, then waited for Kay to begin.

She took a moment to let the atmosphere in the room stew for a few more moments, then opened a manila folder in front of her and withdrew the copy balance sheets.

'Mr Dagenham, when I spoke to you yesterday with your wife, I asked you whether you had any idea who might be targeting boat owners with the vandalism to the windows, and subsequently the recent arson attacks that left one man dead. Is there anything you'd like to tell me before we begin?'

Confusion clouded the man's eyes. 'I, no. Like what?'

'I understand you were seriously ill last year, and that the business experienced a downturn in trade, is that correct?' Kay spun around the documents and laid them out before him. 'Quite a considerable downturn, wasn't it?

He nodded. 'My cancer treatment took over our lives for a few months. It's the busiest time of year for us usually, from June through to September. But I couldn't work – not like that. I managed to do odd jobs here and there, but we had to delve into the savings more than once.'

'You must be relieved that things are picking up again, what with all the repairs to broken windows and the like since these acts of vandalism started targeting the boating community.'

'Well, I… I suppose so. It'd be better if the attacks weren't happening at all, but if we can—'

'Take advantage?' Kay leaned back. 'Tell me about the recent order you received from Jared White.'

'Nothing to it, really. His insurers phoned him last week to say they were going to pay out his claim in full. He was lucky – he'd already passed the sixty-day period when they wouldn't have paid. So he wants me to source him a replacement boat.'

'You're not building it?'

Morris shook his head. 'As I said, those days

are over for me. I always traded in secondhand boats before I got cancer – it's useful to top up the coffers in between the bespoke work, and now it'll be one of my bigger income earners. It certainly pays more than doing repairs.'

He gave a nervous chuckle, which Kay and Sharp ignored.

Instead, Kay flicked through her notes before looking him in the eye. 'How come you caught that teenager who graffitied Sam's boat on your CCTV cameras, but nobody who might've been responsible for the windows being smashed before that?'

The man's cheeks coloured. 'Our system's been on the blink. Some sort of network glitch. I don't know why – I've been onto their technical support lot on and off for the past seven weeks trying to get a response out of them but they keep telling me the fault's at our end.'

'Are you turning off the cameras before breaking the windows?'

'What?' Morris turned to the duty solicitor, who kept a wary gaze on Kay. 'Why would I break anyone's windows?'

Kay ignored his question and instead turned to one of the witness statements on file. 'It seems to me, Mr Dagenham, that every time our victims' boats were attacked, your business stood to benefit.'

'We just provided the cheapest quote, that's all.'

'Is that all? Did you instigate the damage so

that people had to come to you? Did you target people who couldn't afford the full replacement value of their homes even after an insurance payout? Did you take one look at your accounts for this year and decide you needed to take drastic steps to rescue your business?'

'No, no – that's not what happened.'

'Why burn their boats, Mr Dagenham? Their homes. Why did you kill Sam Donaldson? Did he suspect what you were doing?'

'That's not true!' Morris beat his fist on the table, making the duty solicitor jump.

She straightened her suit jacket, placed her hand on his arm, and murmured in his ear.

He sniffed, then wiped the back of his hand under his nose.

'I didn't attack those people, or their boats,' he said, eyes reddening. 'I never would, not after what I've been through this past year. I don't know why people came to us to get their boats fixed, I just do the work that's needed.'

'Then who did provide these people with quotes?'

'You'll have to speak to my wife,' he replied. 'She deals with all the marketing and accounting stuff. I just fix boats.'

FOURTEEN

Two hours later, Louise Dagenham turned away from the duty solicitor appointed to her when Kay and Sharp walked into interview room three and took their seats.

The man beside her handed over business cards, then spoke his name for the recording once Sharp had made the introductions and read out the formal caution.

'Why am I here?' Louise asked. 'Where's Morris? What's going on?'

'Mrs Dagenham, I'd like to ask you some questions,' Kay began. 'As DS Sharp has indicated, this is a formal interview.'

'Okay, but—'

'When I visited your boatyard yesterday, both you and your husband told me that you had no idea who might be involved in the vandalism and arson attacks on local boat owners. I also understand from speaking with several witnesses to the three fires that have occurred in the past six weeks that you've shown a keen interest in the owners and neighbouring vessels, even before the fires happened.' Kay looked up from her notes. 'In fact, you've been in close contact with boat owners at each location for months. Why?'

'Well, whoever's doing this could target us next, couldn't they? I was just trying to find out what was going on. Your lot weren't doing anything. I mean, what would happen if whoever's doing this decides it's not enough to petrol bomb a boat and attacks our boatyard instead?'

'I think that highly unlikely, Mrs Dagenham.' Kay took an evidence bag from Sharp, noticing the slight nod he gave her. She broke open the seal with a flourish. 'Do you recognise this?'

Louise's mouth turned into an "o" of shock. 'Where did you get that?'

'From your office at the boatyard. You'll recall that when I arrived there with my uniformed colleagues this morning I informed you that we had a warrant to search the premises.'

Kay opened the accounting ledger. 'Is this your writing, Mrs Dagenham?'

'How did you get that? It's kept in the safe…'

'Your husband was good enough to give us the combination code an hour ago. Is this your writing?'

Louise paled. 'Yes.'

'Unusual for a business these days to keep manual records. Doesn't your accountant prefer you to use an online system?'

'We do.'

'Then why have this as well?'

'It's… it's just the way I prefer to do things. As a back-up, in case the system fails.'

'So, if I get a warrant to demand your accountant hand over a copy of your current online transactions, this book will match those will it?'

Louise said nothing.

'Or,' Kay continued, 'will I find some extracurricular activities recorded in this that your accountant – and the taxman – are unaware of? Like the cash that was also found in the safe. All fifteen thousand pounds of it.'

'Look, maybe one or two minor jobs, that's all.' Louise turned to the duty solicitor. 'Everyone does that now and again, don't they?'

'I spoke to Jared White before I walked in here,' said Kay. 'He confirms that he never spoke to Morris after his boat was vandalised, and in fact, it was you who approached him. He said you were most insistent that he didn't give the work to one of the larger boatyards, and that you told him they were turning away work because they were too busy.'

'I was just trying to be neighbourly.'

'He doesn't live anywhere near Porter's Lock.'

'It's a community though, isn't it? All these boat people. They like to stick together.'

'They do indeed, Mrs Dagenham. Did you provide the quote to Jared after his boat was destroyed in the fire?'

'Yes.'

'I understand you visited Jared at his

daughter's house where he was staying and doorstepped him into accepting it.' Kay watched as the woman's jaw clenched. 'He said he felt guilty, especially after you explained about Morris's illness.'

'I was just trying to help.'

'Who?'

'Morris. Us.'

Kay closed the ledger and folded her hands on the hardback cover. 'Louise, it's time to tell the truth. This has gone too far. Did you deliberately vandalise boats to ensure a steady stream of work for your boatyard?'

'No comment,' Louise murmured.

'Did you – when it transpired that the income from repairs wasn't enough – then escalate to arson, and petrol bomb Jared White's boat so you could secure a finder's fee for a replacement?'

'No comment.'

Kay handed the ledger back to Sharp and watched as he re-sealed the evidence bag and added his signature. She took a deep breath before asking her next question.

'Mrs Dagenham... Louise... Why did you murder Sam Donaldson? Was it because he refused to have his windows replaced by Morris? Was it revenge?'

Louise blinked. 'How did you know we didn't fix his windows?'

'Our witness recalled that although Sam got a quote from you, he ended up having them replaced by another supplier – one based in Maidstone. Is that why you killed him? Did rage get the better of you?'

'No…' Louise's face crumpled. 'He wasn't meant to die.'

A shocked silence followed her words, and Kay could almost hear the whirring of the recording equipment under the sound of the woman's sobs.

'What happened, Louise?'

'He was meant to escape like Jared did. I didn't know he was sleeping on the sofa in the main cabin, not the bedroom.'

Kay bit back bile. 'You threw the petrol bomb into the living area, didn't you?'

The woman nodded.

'Why didn't you go back and try to rescue him?'

'What was the point? It was too late for him. The flames were too much, and the smoke…' Louise raised her gaze and sniffed. 'I felt so stupid. I'd just lost us a sale.'

FIFTEEN

'Bloody hell, she's a cold one.'

Christie squinted against a low sun and held up his hand to a passing patrol car as he walked beside Kay along the main street.

They had left the station together, Sharp's congratulatory speech still echoing in Kay's ears, and her spirits lifted by Blake Travis being the first to shake her hand.

'I owe you an apology,' he'd said.

'Accepted.' She'd smiled, and tipped her can of beer against his before mingling with the rest of her colleagues.

Now, she huffed her fringe from her eyes and loosened her scarf.

There was a warmth to the air this evening, a promise of spring finally on the breeze, and she inhaled deeply as they crossed the River Medway. Farther along the watercourse, a cabin cruiser slowly floated out of the town's reaches and towards the country park, its passengers clutching wine glasses and their laughter carrying back to where she stood.

'So, I take it her husband didn't have a clue what she was up to?' Christie paused a few paces away, waiting.

'No.' She caught up with him and snorted. 'I don't know whether it was naïvety on his part or whether his whole focus was on his health, but he was shocked when we showed him the ledger – and the footage Lisa Nash subsequently found of Louise leaving the scene of Briony's boat after she set it alight. Travis managed to obtain CCTV footage from a convenience store down the road from the moorings that shows Louise getting into her car. She really did think she'd got away with it.'

'Again.' He stood to one side to let an elderly man on a mobility scooter pass, then shot her a bashful look. 'Sadie's parents had the kids over last night so we had the place to ourselves. I didn't get a chance to tell you earlier.'

Casting a sideways glance at him, Kay noted the faint smile on his lips. 'Well? How did it go, then? Did you ask her?'

'I did.'

'And?'

His smile widened, and she gave him a playful punch on the arm.

'Spill it, Christie. Do I have to buy a new dress or what?'

'She said yes.' His voice held a note of wonder. 'Sadie said yes.'

Kay whooped, gave the taller detective a brief

hug, and set off once more. 'Congratulations. Although can I just say, I told you she would?'

'I know.' The smile was still in his voice. 'The kids were happy too when we told them this morning. Mind you, I think in Charlotte's case, that's just because she gets to invite her best friend. Or perhaps choose the flowers for the bridesmaids' bouquet. Hard to tell with a six-year-old sometimes. Oh, by the way – I overheard Sharp on the phone before we left. Sounds like the recruitment freeze is going to be lifted for a few months. That means new opportunities.'

'Oh.'

'You don't sound too happy about it.'

'New opportunities sometimes means moving on, doesn't it?'

'Maidstone calling, perhaps? You'd do well there.'

'I don't know…'

'You'll see. Don't underestimate yourself, Kay. It'd be a good move for you.'

'But I like it here.' She heard the panic in her voice. 'I like working with all of you.'

'Don't worry – it might not be for a while.' He smiled. 'After all, there's a few people in line for promotion ahead of us at the moment anyway. But I'll bet they ask you one day.'

'Maybe.' Kay jerked her chin towards a side street. 'Okay, this is me. See you in the morning?'

'Seven fifteen on the dot. According to Sharp, he wants a full debrief at eight so we'll pick up some decent coffee on the way in if you like.'

'Sounds good. See you.'

Despite the anticipation of having to relocate, Kay took a moment to reflect on the past week and the result the team had got. She would never accept it as her win, not with the amount of manpower it took to collate all the witness statements and carry out the searches – and the work wasn't over yet.

But for now, there was a lightness to her step and she hummed under her breath as she realised there was a decent bottle of chardonnay waiting in the refrigerator at home.

She stopped when she turned the corner into the road where she lived.

Parked outside her block of flats was a scruffy, mud-clad four-by-four.

Standing next to it was a man with dark curly hair dressed in jeans and a suit jacket, and he was smiling at her.

'Adam,' she said, hurrying over. 'I'm so sorry – I know I was meant to call you back, but we had a breakthrough, and…'

He grinned and pulled her into a hug before kissing her. 'I heard. Well done.'

'Thank you. Who—'

'Someone called Lisa Nash told me when I phoned to speak to you. You'd already left though.'

'Lisa… She's such a gossip.'

'In the best possible sense.' He kissed her nose. 'Fancy a celebratory dinner tonight?'

'Sounds like a great idea.' Kay grinned. 'And

I've heard about a really good gastro pub not too far away from here.'

THE END

ABOUT THE AUTHOR

Rachel Amphlett is a USA Today bestselling author of crime fiction and spy thrillers, many of which have been translated worldwide.

Her novels are available in eBook, print, and audiobook formats from libraries and retailers as well as her website shop.

A keen traveller, Rachel has both Australian and British citizenship.

Find out more about Rachel's books at: www.rachelamphlett.com.